SAY HEY!

A Song of Willie Mays

by PETER MANDEL ★ Illustrated by DON TATE

Jump at the Sun Hyperion Books for Children

For Bill O'Hara and Dusty Rhodes.
—*P. M.*
Thank God for my mom, my biggest fan, best supporter,
and most enthusiastic cheerleader.
—*D. T.*

Visit www.jumpatthesun.com, a part of the Network

Printed in Singapore.
FIRST EDITION
1 3 5 7 9 10 8 6 4 2

This book is set in 19-point Memphis.
The art was executed in acrylics.

Library of Congress Cataloging-in-Publication Data:
Mandel, Peter, 1957–
Say hey!: a song of Willie Mays/Peter Mandel: illustrated by Don Tate.—1st ed.
p. cm.
Summary: Rhyming text tells the story of Willie Mays, from his childhood in Alabama
to his triumphs in baseball and his acquisition of the nickname, the "Say Hey Kid."
ISBN 0-7868-0480-7 (trade).-ISBN 0-7868-2417-4 (lib.)
1. Mays, Willie, 1931– Juvenile literature. 2. Baseball players—United States—Biography
Juvenile literature. [1. Mays, Willie, 1931– . 2. Baseball Players. 3. Afro-Americans—Biography.]
I. Tate, Don, ill. II. Title. III. Title: Song of Willie Mays.
GV865.M389M35 2000
796.357'092—dc21
[B]   99-34441

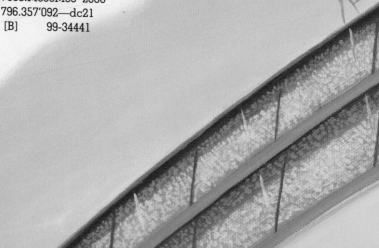

You were born in Alabama,
where the land lies flat.

Say hey, Willie. Say hey.

And your daddy worked the steel mill
(though he sure could swing a bat).

Say hey, Willie. Say hey.

Then you grew up not so tall,
an' there ain't no changin' that.

Say hey, Willie. Say hey.

So you played a little ball?
In the Negro Leagues was all.

Say hey, Willie. Say hey.

When the Giants sent a scout
Wasn't you they meant to call.

Say hey, Willie. Say hey.

Yeah, they signed you to a year . . .
(hope you're still here in the fall).

Say hey, Willie. Say hey.

'Cause you're nothin' but a kid
with a smooth, smooth swing.

Say hey, Willie. Say hey.

But to swing for the Giants
is a whole 'nother thing.

Say hey, Willie. Say hey.

Well, I guess you made the team.
But it's early in the spring.

Say hey, Willie. Say hey.

Hear you whiffed a steady breeze
until the crowd began to shout . . .

Say hey, Willie. Say hey.

But then, **Kaa-RACK!!**,
you smoked some singles
an' you threw some runners out....

Say hey, Willie. Say hey.

Hear you're Rookie of the Year.
Man, I never had a doubt!

Say hey, Willie. Say hey.

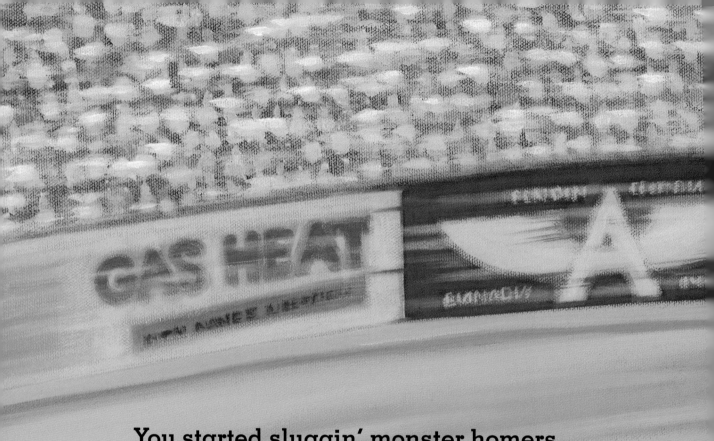

You started sluggin' monster homers
that only you could chase. . . .

Say hey, Willie. Say hey.

You started roarin' 'round the bases
like you were in a great big race. . . .

Say hey, Willie. Say hey.

And when you drove in Giant runs
you grew a smile on your face!

Say hey, Willie. Say hey.

Say, what was that they yelled
each time you'd make the pitcher pay?

Say hey, Willie. Say hey.

Say, what was that new nickname,
which sounded better than "hooray"?

Say hey, Willie. Say hey.

Say, *what*? The *Say Hey Kid* is
what they call you to this day!

Say hey, Willie. Say hey.

Now it's 1954,
and you stole the batting crown.

Say hey, Willie. Say hey.

Now you're makin' basket catches
as your cap comes flyin' down.

Say hey, Willie. Say hey.

Now you made the best grab ever.
Now you're *mayor* of this town.

Say hey, Willie. Say hey.

It doesn't matter, Willie Mays,
that you ain't no six-foot-two.

Say hey, Willie. Say hey.

It just don't matter, Willie Mays,
that I'm a poor kid just like you.

Say hey, Willie. Say hey.

It doesn't matter. You're the best.
There ain't nothin' we can't do!

Say hey, Willie. Say hey.

They say of all the sluggers
who have ever played this game . . .

Say hey, Willie. Say hey.

They say that no one ever hit
or ran or threw the same. . . .

Say hey, Willie. Say hey.

They say that you're the *greatest*
in the Baseball Hall of Fame!

Say hey, Willie Mays . . .

Say hey.

Say Hey Facts

Nicknamed the "Say Hey Kid" because of his boyish enthusiasm, some believe Willie Mays may have been the greatest baseball player who ever lived.

Mays was a speedy center fielder for the New York Giants in the 1950s and later for the San Francisco Giants and the New York Mets. He chased down impossible fly balls and snared them, often in his famous "basket catch" with his glove at waist level. When running for the catch, his cap came flying off so frequently some people thought he wore a cap that was a couple of sizes too big—just for dramatic effect. In the 1954 World Series, Mays made what is considered the best catch of all time, grabbing a 460-foot fly ball hit by Vic Wertz of the Cleveland Indians, and whirling to throw the ball back to the infield in a single motion. This famous catch helped the Giants go on to win the series in four games.

Mays was born to a poor family in rural Alabama. While playing for the Birmingham Black Barons, a local Negro League team, he was discovered by accident when the New York Giants sent a scout to look at one of Mays's teammates. Only 5'11" and 170 pounds, Mays was still a powerful hitter. To this day, he remains in third place among baseball's greatest home run hitters (after Hank Aaron and Babe Ruth). His unique blend of base-stealing, fielding, and slugging ability has yet to be matched.